P9-CQV-441

TRINITY SCHOOL
ELLICOTT CITY, MD

WITHDRAWN

J I M M Y   C A R T E R

The Little Baby
Snoogle-Fleejer

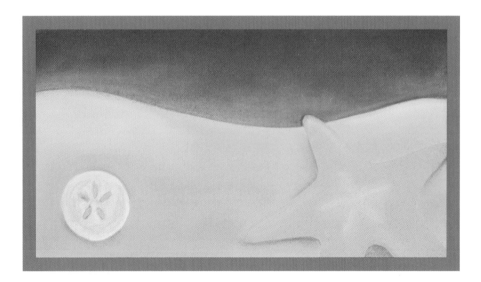

I L L U S T R A T E D   B Y   **A** M Y   **C** A R T E R

TIMES **B**OOKS
NEW YORK

WITHDRAWN
TRINITY SCHOOL
ELLICOTT CITY, MD

For Jamie, Maggie, Jeremy, and Joshua
–J.C.

To Jim, our cats, and Benito in Seattle
–A.C.

Copyright © 1995 by Jimmy Carter and Amy Carter

All rights reserved under International and Pan-American Copyright Conventions.
Published in the United States by Times Books, a division of Random House, Inc., New York,
and simultaneously in Canada by Random House of Canada Limited, Toronto.

Library of Congress Cataloging-in-Publication Data

Carter, Jimmy
The little baby Snoogle-Fleejer / Jimmy Carter; illustrated by Amy Carter. –1st ed.
      p.   cm.
    Summary: When all of the other children run off at the sight of a terrifying sea monster,
Jeremy, who is unable to walk, discovers a kindred lonely spirit in the baby Snoogle-Fleejer.
    ISBN 0-8129-2731-1
[1. Sea monsters–Fiction. 2. Physically handicapped–Fiction. 3. Friendship–Fiction.]
I. Carter, Amy, ill. II. Title.
PZ7.C2455Li   1996   [E]–dc20   95-41408

Manufactured in the United States of America

9 8 7 6 5 4 3 2

First Edition

Book design by Edward Miller

Once upon a time there was a little boy named Jeremy who lived with his mother in a small house near the sea. His mother earned a bare living for the two of them by washing clothes for some of the wealthy families in their town. Jeremy loved her very much, and was proud when he could help with chores around their home.

Being crippled, Jeremy was not able to run and play with other children, but he could move around using his crutches. He enjoyed reading and studying and was a happy child.

One of Jeremy's favorite places was on some big rocks near the beach, in a spot that was protected from the strong ocean breezes and usually warmed by the sunshine. His mother had taught Jeremy to swim when he was quite young, and he enjoyed being in the water. He limped slowly when he was on the shore, but he felt free and at home in the waves.

The other children often played on the beach, and he would watch them at their games. They never asked him to join them, and sometimes one of the larger boys would try to make him cry by teasing him about moving so slowly and not being able to play tag or chase a ball. However, he was a brave lad, sure of his mother's love, and was content even though he could not join in the children's games.

One summer day Jeremy was watching the other children playing volleyball on the beach when suddenly there was a commotion in the sea.

Something large and strange was approaching them, appearing every now and then above the surface of the water. "It must be porpoises!" "It could be a whale!"

All of a sudden an enormous head came out of the waves, and the frightened children screamed, "It's a sea monster!"

They all ran away as fast as they could. All except Jeremy. He reached for his crutches, but one of them slid off the rock and fell on the sand just as the strange creature was coming out of the ocean.

The monster's eyes were as big as softballs, its ears hung down like large burlap bags, there were spines on top of its head and down its back, and there seemed to be a hundred huge teeth in the gaping mouth. The beast was horribly ugly and frightening, but strangely, he seemed to be smiling!

Jeremy was almost too frightened to move, and could only wait to be eaten as the monster drew closer.

"Don't be afraid," the creature said, "I'm not going to hurt you."

Jeremy was so amazed to hear these words, or any words at all, that he stopped scrambling for his crutch. Finally he was able to talk. "Who are you? What are you? Where did you come from? How did you get so large? Why are you here? What do you want?"

His questions poured out, and the monster laughed. "Wait just a minute, and give me a chance to answer. My home is deep in the sea. I am a baby Snoogle-Fleejer, very small compared to my parents. They have always warned me to come near the shore only in very lonely places. I have slipped away a few times to see if I could find a friend, but people always run away when they see me. You are the only one who has ever waited for me to get close enough to talk. You must be very brave. Would you like to play?"

"I would have run, too," said Jeremy, "but I dropped my crutch. I don't have many friends either, and I can't play because I'm crippled."

"Would you like to go for a ride? There will be a lot of people coming in a few minutes, and they might want to harm me, but we would be safe at sea. I'll be careful and bring you back after a while."

Jeremy climbed onto the monster's head, and the little baby Snoogle-Fleejer moved carefully out through the waves. They swam along near the shore. They asked each other a lot of questions and enjoyed each other's company.

Finally Jeremy told his new friend that he had to go home. He didn't want his mother to worry. "Okay," said the Snoogle-Fleejer. "Would you like another ride tomorrow?"

They agreed that only his mother should know about his strange experience.

Jeremy rushed home all excited. But when he tried to tell his mother what had happened, she interrupted him. "Hush, Jeremy, I'm busy, and don't want to hear any more. Your imagination is running away with you. Maybe you have been reading too many books."

Taken aback, Jeremy decided to keep his secret to himself.

Jeremy found time to meet his new friend often, and they had great times together in the sea. Sometimes they would even go under the water for a short time, with the boy holding tightly to the Snoogle-Fleejer's big ears.

It was a happy time for both of them.

One day Jeremy returned home and was surprised to find his mother sitting quietly in her rocking chair. He noticed that her work was not finished, and he asked if anything was wrong.

"Yes, Jeremy," she replied. "I have always been honest with you, and there is no reason now not to tell the truth. I'm sorry I haven't been patient with you. For several weeks I have been sick. The doctor told me that I am very ill. The operation that I need would cost a lot of money, and I have been able to earn only enough to pay our bills. I just don't know what we can do."

Jeremy tried to comfort his mother. He promised to help her more around the house. The boy was so busy taking care of his mother that he had no time to visit with the baby Snoogle-Fleejer. Despite their best efforts, his mother became weaker as the days went by, spending more and more time in bed.

TRINITY SCHOOL
ELLICOTT CITY, MD

One afternoon, when his mother was resting quietly, Jeremy returned to his favorite rock. A few tears were running down his cheeks when the baby Snoogle-Fleejer saw him sitting on the shore.

"What's the matter?" the Snoogle-Fleejer asked. "It's been a long time since I've seen you. Why are you crying?"

Jeremy explained that his mother was ill, and that they did not have any money to pay for the operation she needed. "I wish there was something I could do."

"What's money?" asked the baby Snoogle-Fleejer. "Maybe I can help."

Jeremy tried to explain and finally took a few copper coins out of his pocket to show his friend. "We need much more than this, though."

"Do they have to be this color?" asked the monster.

"No, silver coins are worth more, and gold ones are much more valuable."

"Come with me," said the baby Snoogle-Fleejer.

They moved out into the deep water, then far down the coast until they reached some sharp rocks.

"Wait here," the baby Snoogle-Fleejer said, and he dove under while Jeremy swam around on the surface. He returned after a few minutes and the boy took his usual perch on his friend's head. They swam silently to shore.

After Jeremy climbed off, the monster opened his mouth, and dropped a number of gold coins onto the sand.

Jeremy gasped in surprise.

"Would these be helpful?" the baby Snoogle-Fleejer asked. "There is a large chest full of them in an old wrecked ship on the bottom of the sea."

Putting the coins deep in his pocket, Jeremy hurried home as fast as he could. He showed his mother the treasure. She had never seen so much money in her life and asked Jeremy a hundred questions. He told her all about the baby Snoogle-Fleejer and their many adventures together. She no longer questioned his story.

They were both so happy. Now she could have the operation.

After his mother was well again, Jeremy took her to meet his monster friend. She wanted to thank him for helping. They all became friends and enjoyed many seagoing trips together. Jeremy soon became a hero among the other children, who saw him riding on the little baby Snoogle-Fleejer's head.

"It's unbelievable," they said. "Jeremy is really strong and brave. All by himself he has tamed a ferocious sea monster!"

TRINITY SCHOOL
ELLICOTT CITY, MD

WITHDRAWN